niles!

Gertie's Big Mouth

more adventures from the Bahamas!!

Heather Rand

August 2015

Written by **Heather Rand**

Illustrated by **Bernadette Chamberlain**

Author: Heather Rand
Illustrator: Bernadette Chamberlain
Digital Layout: Erik Jenson

©*2014*
ISBN: 978-0-9877560-2-2

For my cruising friends, Doug & Connie formerly on s/v High Stepper, who pushed me to do something with my stories. For my husband and captain, Murray. Thank you so much for your years of love and encouragement. And, last but not least, for my new grandchild due to arrive in March. I love you all!

Everyone in the Bahamas knows that groupers have very large mouths but no other grouper uses hers quite as much as Gertie. And she was using it to get into trouble once more.

"I know where there is some buried treasure," said Gertie brightly. "Well, it isn't buried now, but it was." Oh, no, thought Gertie, what have I done now? Will I ever learn to keep my mouth shut?

But, it was much too late. The whole school had heard her and all five of the blue runners turned and stared at her.

"I want to see!"

"Let's go!"

"Me too!"

"I don't believe it."

"I'll believe it when I see it!" Their voices came all at once, tumbling over each other.

Defiantly, Gertie stated, "It is true. I saw it just last week and.....". The other fish interrupted her, demanding to be taken to see "the treasure". The blue runners followed Gertie as she dodged from reef to coral head and on to some swaying purple fan coral. Although she was in a hurry, Gertie always kept her eyes looking around for danger. There could be a shark or a barracuda nearby, and they would love a tasty morsel of young grouper.

Finally, she reached the underwater canyon where she had last seen the treasure. Holding her breath, she peered over the edge. "Whew, it is still there", she whispered to herself. "Here it is," she announced to the other fish. "Come and see."

The others followed her over the edge of the canyon and encircled the object that Gertie was hovering over.

"That isn't a treasure!" said Bobby Blue.

"No, it is just garbage!" scoffed Betty Blue.

"It isn't just garbage!" asserted Gertie, "It IS a treasure! You don't ever find blue bottles. I see brown ones, clear ones and even green ones sometimes. But, not very often do you find a blue one! And, look it is not even broken. In fact, the cork is still in it. Do you think perhaps there is a message in this bottle? Maybe someone needs our help." She looked around but all of the other fish had gone. "It IS a treasure," she mumbled, "and maybe there IS a message." But there was no one there to hear.

Later, back at the reef, Gertie explained to her mother what had happened. "Momma, they don't believe me!" she cried as she finished her tale.

"Gertie," her mother admonished gently, "what have I said about telling stories that are not quite true?"

"But, Momma..."

"No, dear, listen to me. If you continue to tell these tall tales, no one will believe anything you say". And Gertie promised she would try to do better.

About a week later, Gertie was swimming with her friend, Penny, a goat who lived on a nearby island. Penny was quite excited and worried at the same time. "Gertie," Penny said, "Did you hear about the big storm that is coming?"

"What big storm?" asked Gertie.

"Everyone is talking about it. Cecilia heard about it from some people on the beach. The pigs have gathered some extra food and even the goats have brought some branches and leaves into the cave where we spend the night. The storm is supposed to arrive later tomorrow and I wanted to warn you, so you too could get ready," explained Penny.

Gertie thanked her and immediately returned to her home on the reef. There she gathered all of the reef residents together and told them about the storm. "It is going to be very bad," she said. "The people on the islands as well as the pigs and goats are all getting prepared. We should get ready too."

So, the fish and other critters on the reef got to work. They tidied up the entrances to their homes, dragged away the shells lying around and trimmed some of the overhanging soft corals. Some even stashed a little extra food. Then they waited. And waited. And waited.

On land, the storm blew in just as expected. The wind howled through the palm trees as the lightning flashed and the rain pelted down. But, down below on the reef, nothing changed. Oh, maybe the current was a little stronger and that made it harder to swim in certain directions. And the water wasn't as perfectly clear as usual. But otherwise, none of the fish or critters even noticed the storm raging above them.

The next day, a delegation of fish came to Gertie's home. "Gertie, you must stop this telling of tales! Look at all of the work we went to and there was NO storm."

Gertie hung her head in shame as she said, "But it was true; Penny told me..."

The other fish did not want to listen to her explanation. "Don't do it again or you may have to find a different reef to call home."

After the angry fish had left, Gertie's mom tried to comfort her. But she also said, "Maybe now you will watch what you say to others."

"Mom, there WAS a storm," argued Gertie.

"Maybe there was," said her mom, "but it didn't affect us down here. That is the important thing to remember. Make sure your facts are right before you tell others what to do."

"OK, I have learned my lesson," agreed Gertie quietly. "I will not tell any more stories."

And for a few weeks, she didn't.

But Gertie had a wonderful imagination and loved to share her thoughts with others. It wasn't a huge problem though, as these were just small stories and all the other fish in the school knew that she was just being Gertie.

One day, Gertie wandered quite far from her home reef. It was time to turn around and swim back to where she belonged when she heard a weak cry.

"Help me!"

Where did that come from? Gertie scanned the area around her but saw nothing.

"Help me."

She heard it again. Swimming slowly, Gertie headed further towards the channel into the deep water. This was dangerous water for Gertie as big fish and sharks might be found here.

Gertie peered around, looking for the source of the cry but also watching for danger.

"Help me, please!"

The cry was louder now. Was there something near the edge of that wrecked boat? Gertie took one look and jumped back, prepared to swim for her life. It was a shark!

"Please come back and help me," the voice pleaded. Gertie peeked over the boat once again. Yep, it was a shark all right but he was trapped somehow. Gertie took a longer look now.

"What is your problem?" she asked.

"I am tangled in this fishing line and cannot move. Please can you help me?"

"But, you are a SHARK and I am afraid of sharks!" said Gertie.

"Oh, but I am just a nurse shark and you don't need to be afraid of me. I will never hurt you."

"I am just a little grouper? What can I do to help?" asked Gertie.

"I don't know, "said the shark," but I DO know that if I don't get untangled before the tide turns, I will die.

"How come?" asked Gertie.

"Sharks need to swim, so that the water flows through their gills, to allow them to breathe. I am just lucky that the current is moving fast enough here to give me the flow of water that I need. But, I don't have much time!"

"Hang on!" exclaimed Gertie, "I will be right back!"

Gertie swam as fast as she could back to her home. She didn't take the time to dodge from coral patch to purple fan coral or even to a small reef. She just swam straight home. Once she got there, she yelled as loud as she could. "Everyone, I need help!" Heads popped out all over the reef to see what was the trouble.

"Oh, it is just Gertie, up to her usual tricks!" And they started to go back into their holes.

"Wait!" yelled Gertie, " I really need some help. There is a shark.."

"Where?"

"Nearby?"

"Oh, no, are you hurt?" Everyone was talking at once.

"Please listen," cried Gertie, "He isn't a dangerous shark but he will die if we don't all help him." Finally, the reef quieted down and the fish and the critters all listened to what Gertie had to say. At first, they didn't believe her. Maybe this was just another of her stories. But Gertie insisted that she was telling the truth and that there really was a shark that needed their help. Eventually all of the fish and critters agreed to help and Gertie quickly led them to wrecked boat and the trapped shark.

"We are here!" she called, "Are you still ok?"

The shark answered, "Yes, but I don't have much more time. You will have to be quick. How will you cut the fishing line?"

Gertie smiled and said, "I brought help!" Just then the rest of the reef's residents popped their heads over the wreck. Immediately Charlie the Crab tackled the fishing line while Larry the Lobster worked another piece of the line against his sharp spines. Polly the Parrotfish used her small but sharp mouth to bite at the line as well. Gertie couldn't do much but watch as all of her friends got to work.

Eventually the shark was free of the line. But, he still didn't move. "What is the matter now?" asked Gertie.

"The lines seem to have damaged one of my pectoral fins. You know, the fins on the side?"

"Of course, I know what a pectoral fin is." stated Gertie, "After all, I am a fish too!"

"Right, I should have known," said the shark as he rolled his eyes. "But, it is very sore and I cannot move it."

The doctorfish swam over and took a look at the
damaged fin. "It is badly cut and will need tending.
We must get him back to our reef where I can look
after him."

A passing Loggerhead turtle offered to tow the shark
to the reef, using a piece of rope that Gertie had found
near the wreck. "Grab on with your mouth and hold
tight," yelled the turtle as he started to swim.

Eventually the shark was safely settled near the home
reef. The current here wasn't as strong but enough
water flowed to allow him to rest his fins. The doctorfish examined the sore joint and finally said, "I think
that you will lose one part of the fin. But the rest will
be just fine in time. If you want, you can stay here, on
our reef, until you heal."

The shark thanked everyone very much, especially his new friend Gertie. "We haven't even been introduced yet," he said. "My name is Stephen."

"I am so happy to meet you," answered Gertie as she introduced herself, "and I am so glad that everyone believed me and came to help you".

"Not half as glad as I am!" laughed Stephen.

Later Gertie was telling Penny all about the adventure with Stephen, the shark. "And that IS a true story!" said Gertie. "I have learned my lesson. When I make up a story, I will make sure that everyone knows it is made-up. Then they will believe me when I tell them something true."

Penny asked innocently, "Have you ever thought about writing a book? You have such a great imagination! Maybe you could write this story about Stephen, the shark, and how he was rescued?"

Slowly Gertie swam away, wondering if a fish could really write a book?'

Maybe she could.

And just maybe she did.

The End

CPSIA information can be obtained at www.ICGtesting.com
Printed in the USA
LVOW01s0702050415

433162LV00004B/11/P